A GOLDEN BOOK • NEW YORK

randomhousekids.com

ISBN 978-0-399-55891-7

T#: 487764

MANUFACTURED IN CHINA

10 9 8 7 6 5 4 3 2 1

MIGHTY MONSTER MACHINES

V*room!* Blaze raced across the countryside.

"Let's head for that hill, Blaze! I bet it would make an awesome jump," said AJ. He was Blaze's best friend—and the best driver a Monster Machine could have.

"Give me some speed!" Blaze cheered. AJ pressed the pedal. They raced up the hill and shot into the air!

Blaze and AJ landed in Axle City.
"Hubcaps! I've never seen so many Monster Machines!" Blaze said. "They're all driving to the Monster Dome to see the big championship race!"
"Let's go get a closer look," said AJ.

Inside the Monster Dome, Blaze and AJ
met Gabby.

"I'm a mechanic," she said. "I fix all the
Monster Machines. Would you like to meet
some of the racers?"

Blaze and AJ met Stripes the tiger truck. He had special claws on his tires that made him great at climbing.

They met Starla, a cowgirl truck who could do rope tricks.

They met Darington,
the amazing stunt truck . . .

and Zeg the dinosaur truck,
who loved to smash
and bash.

"Out of my way! Me first, me first!" said a big truck as he pushed past the others.

"His name is Crusher," Gabby said. "He thinks he's the best racer ever."

A small truck named Pickle pulled up next to Crusher. "I cannot wait to see who will win the big race," Pickle said. "It could be anyone!"

"No, Pickle—it's going to be me, me, me!" announced Crusher. Then he whispered to himself, "Because I'm going to cheat!"

A hatch on Crusher's side opened, and his Trouble Bubble Wand popped out. It blew big bubbles that captured Darington, Starla, Stripes, Zeg, and even Blaze. They began to float away.

The bubbles floated across the countryside. When Blaze's bubble finally popped, he landed in the Badlands, far from Axle City. Stripes landed nearby—but he was stuck in some vines hanging from a cliff!

"Gaskets!" Blaze exclaimed. "We have to get to Stripes fast!"

Blaze saw that the rocks were shaped like ramps.

He and AJ jumped from one to the other. The steeper the ramp, the higher they went!

Finally, they reached the top and saved Stripes.

As the trucks rolled through a forest, Grizzly Trucks started to chase them. They had to escape, but the only way out was cut off by a river.

Blaze thought for a moment. "To get across, we need something we can float on."

The trucks found a rock and a piece of wood and
pushed them into the water. The rock sank right away.

"But the wood is floating!" Blaze said. "We can get
across on it!"

The trucks jumped onto the wood and floated to the
other side of the river.

The trucks sped along a snowy mountainside. They saw Zeg just as his bubble popped. He fell to the ground and tumbled down a steep, icy hill.

"Let's *blaaaze!*" shouted AJ and Blaze. They raced down the hill and caught Zeg at the edge of the cliff with Blaze's tow hook.

"Zeg so happy!" Zeg cheered. "Blaze save Zeg!"

There was one last Monster Machine to find! The trucks drove through a cave and found Starla at the bottom of a hole.

"We'll get you out!" Blaze shouted down to her.

Luckily, two buckets were hanging from a pulley nearby. Starla climbed into the lower bucket. The trucks filled the other bucket with heavy things. When their bucket grew heavier than Starla's, it went down and Starla's bucket rose up and out of the hole!

The trucks zoomed back to the Monster Dome.
They arrived just as the race was about to start.
"Good luck out there," Blaze said.
"You should be in the race, too," Stripes said.

Blaze was amazed. "You really want me to race with you?"

"Blaze *friend*!" Zeg said.

"All right!" Blaze cheered. "AJ and I will do it together!"

"And they're off!" said Bump Bumperman, the announcer. The Monster Machines revved and roared and raced around the track.

But Crusher didn't want anyone else to win. One by one, he tried to knock the other racers out of his way, but there was one racer he couldn't get past.

"Let's *blaaaze*!" Blaze accelerated and
sped across the finish line.

"We won!" AJ cheered.

"No! It's just not fair," Crusher whined.
"I wanted to win. Me! Me! Me!"

"Blaze! You're the Monster Machine World Champion," Bump Bumperman said. "What will you do next?"

"I'd like to hang out with my new friends," Blaze said.

The Monster Machines cheered as they took a victory lap around the track with their new friend, Blaze.

One morning at the Axle City Garage,
Blaze and AJ were helping their friend
Gabby unload a shipment of tires.

"They're silly tires!" Gabby explained
with a giggle.

Inside the crates were dancing tires . . . stinky tires . . . and even feathery chicken tires!

"*Bok-bok-bok!*" clucked the tires as they rolled away.

Blaze and AJ saw Zeg trying to drive down the street. He was having a hard time because his tires had big holes in them!

Blaze pulled out his towing hook. "Hang on," he said. "I'll give you a tow!"

Suddenly, a crate wiggled and jiggled and then burst open! *Boing! Boing!* Four bright green silly tires bounced out.

"Funny tires go up and down," the dinosaur truck laughed. "Zeg like! Zeg want those tires!"

Zeg put on the tires—and started bouncing!
"Blaze? AJ? We have a problem," said
Gabby. "Those tires are the silliest tires of all!
They're super-bouncy tires. Once they start
bouncing, they don't stop!"

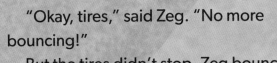

"Okay, tires," said Zeg. "No more bouncing!"

But the tires didn't stop. Zeg bounced out of the garage—and straight into traffic!

"Don't worry, Gabby," said Blaze. "We'll find a way to stop those bouncy tires."

"If we're gonna catch Zeg," said AJ, "we need to use Blazing Speed!"

Blaze revved his engine, popped his boosters, and—*VROOM!*—took off to save his friend!

"I know how we can save Zeg," said Blaze.
"Let's make those bouncy tires stick to the road.
We'll use adhesion! Adhesion is when two things
stick together."

Blaze unrolled a piece of tape and stuck it
right in Zeg's path.

Zeg landed on the tape, but he bounced off
again! The tape was sticky, but not sticky enough.
    "Next time we try adhesion, we need something
even stickier," AJ said.
    Zeg kept bouncing straight toward a building.
    "Uh-oh!" said Blaze. "That's the egg warehouse!"

Zeg crashed through the warehouse, knocking over crates and baskets. "Sorry! Coming through!" he yelled.

The bouncy tires hit a red button. A crane
turned and picked up a huge egg.
"Oh, no!" cried a worker truck. "He just
turned on the Giant Egg Dropper!"

The crane was going to drop the egg, so Blaze
raced as fast as he could to save it. He ducked
under conveyor belts and weaved past fallen
crates and baskets.

When the egg dropped, Blaze reached out
and caught it just in time!

Blaze had saved the giant egg, but he still had to save Zeg.

"We can use adhesion again to stop those tires. Maybe this is sticky enough to work." AJ grabbed a bottle and squeezed out a puddle of glue.

Zeg landed in the glue. The goo splattered all over the tires and slowed Zeg down. But then he sprang up . . . and up . . . and up . . . until— *SNAP!*—he broke free! Just like the tape, the glue couldn't stop his bouncing!

"We're gonna need something even stickier," said AJ.

"Oh, no!" groaned Zeg. The super-bouncy
tires were taking him straight toward a bakery—
and a beautiful frosted cake!
"Somebody stop him!" cried the baker.

"I've got an idea," said Blaze. "What if we use quick-dry cement? That's the super-stickiest thing I can think of!"

Blaze put together a spiral mixing blade, a rotating drum, and a discharge chute, transforming himself into a cement mixer.

"The sticky cement is mixed and ready to pour!" called AJ.

Blaze tipped the discharge chute. Cement flowed out in a goopy gray puddle.

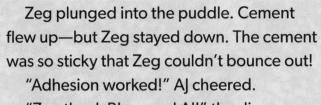

Zeg plunged into the puddle. Cement flew up—but Zeg stayed down. The cement was so sticky that Zeg couldn't bounce out!

"Adhesion worked!" AJ cheered.

"Zeg thank Blaze and AJ!" the dinosaur truck said with a smile.

"You're welcome, big fella!" said Blaze. "Now, what do you say we get you a different set of tires?"

The dinosaur truck nodded. "Zeg like that idea! Zeg like!"

Back at the garage, Gabby replaced the bouncy tires with regular tires. "How do they feel?" she asked.

"*Wheeee!*" Zeg shouted as he cruised around the garage. "No bouncing!"

Blaze and AJ laughed, glad their friend was safely back on the ground!

It was a hot, sunny day, and Blaze
and his buddies were ready to cool off!
They went down to the river to catch a
cool breeze on a sailboat.

"This boat is amazing!" said Gabby.

"Yeah, Blaze! How do you make it go
so fast?" asked Stripes.

"The sailboat moves fast because it's powered by the wind," explained Blaze. "Wind has the power to push things!"

"When wind blows against the sail, it pushes
our boat forward through the water," said Blaze.
"That's wind power!"

"I like it!" growled Stripes as the boat sliced
across the ocean.

Nearby, Crusher and Pickle were
having trouble with their boat.
"Oops," said Pickle as the sail
fell on top of his pal Crusher.
"Ahoy, Crusher! You need
some help?" shouted Blaze.

"Ha! I don't need help," replied Crusher. "Besides, my boat is way faster than yours."

"I don't know, Crusher," said Stripes. "Our boat is pretty fast."

"Oh, yeah? Then let's have a race!" said Crusher.

"Okay, racers," said Gabby.
"On your marks, get set, SAIL!"

With a gust of wind, Blaze
and his friends zipped across
the water. But Crusher's boat
didn't go anywhere.

"Uh-oh, Crusher. I think you're losing," said Pickle.

"Well, looks like there's only one thing I can do to win this race," Crusher announced. *"Cheat."*

"I'm going to make something to knock Blaze's boat right out of my way!" giggled Crusher. "I'll build . . . a Wild Wavemaker!" With the press of a button, the wavemaker began to hum, and the water got rough and choppy.

"Oh, my," said Pickle. "Those are some big waves."

"That ought to stop Blaze," added Crusher.

"Where'd all these waves come from?" asked Blaze as his boat began to rock back and forth.

"It's Crusher!" exclaimed Gabby, pointing at their boat. "He's making them!"

The waves grew so big and rough, they pushed Blaze's boat up onto a beach!

"Whoa. We've landed on a tropical island," observed Blaze.

"And look! Our sailboat is broken!" exclaimed Stripes.

"Our boat is missing some really important pieces," added AJ. "The mast, the mainsheet, and the sail are gone!"

"Without those pieces, we can't use wind power!" said Gabby.

"And that means we can't sail home!" said Stripes.

"Hey, Gabby, if we find the missing parts, can you fix our sailboat?" asked Blaze.

"You bet I can!" replied Gabby. "I can fix anything!"

"Great!" Blaze said. "Then let's go find them!"

Meanwhile, Crusher and Pickle had washed up onto another part of the island.

"Look! Our sailboat is broken!" said Pickle. "But that's okay. You and me, we'll just work together and fix it."

"Oh, all right," replied Crusher. "But let's hurry—I want to sail away before Blaze so we can get home first!"

On the other side of the island, AJ, Blaze, and Stripes found the mast from their boat.

"There it is!" said AJ. "It's on that cliff!"

"How are we gonna get there without falling into that goo?" Blaze wondered aloud.

"I can do it!" said Stripes. But the rocks were too far apart for Stripes to jump. Then Blaze had a better idea!

"Stripes, you can use wind power!" suggested Blaze.
"If you wait until the wind is blowing, it can push you and
help you jump farther!"

Blaze and his friends found the
mainsheet—just as a monkey ran off with it!
"I'll catch him!" Blaze said.
Vroom! Blaze used his rocket boosters
to catch the silly monkey.

After getting the mainsheet back, Blaze and his friends needed one more piece to fix their boat.

"Look! There's our sail!" yelled Stripes.

"It's blowing away!" said Blaze. "C'mon! We're going to need everyone's help!"

Meanwhile, when Crusher saw the sail float by, he got an idea.

"We're going to take that sail and use it for our boat!" he told Pickle.

"Oh, no!" said Stripes. "Crusher is trying to take our sail!"

"We can get to the sail super fast if we use wind power!" replied Blaze. "Let's build a kite so we can fly up and get it!" With that, he changed into a huge glider. "I'm a kite-flying monster machine!"

Using wind power, Blaze and AJ soared to the top of the mountain.

"We've got the sail!" said Blaze. "Let's put it back on our boat so we all can go home!"

"Our boat is fixed!" said Gabby.

"Now we can sail back to Axle City!" cheered Stripes.

"Guess what, slowpokes. I fixed my sailboat first!" Crusher teased—just as his boat began to sink! Blaze and Stripes raced to the rescue.

"Here, grab one of these!" Blaze said, and he threw a couple of life preservers to the splashing trucks.
"Hooray! Blaze saved us!" cheered Pickle.

"Well, at least I can finally relax," grumbled Crusher, snuggling into his life preserver. "Yup, from here on out, it's smooth sailing."

Suddenly, a little crab gave Crusher a pinch!

"*Ow-ow-ow!*" yelped the blue truck.

Blaze and his friends sailed back to Axle City for more adventures!